FRANKIE'S
MAGIC
FOOTBALL

BY FRANK LAMPARD

FRANKIE'S MAGIC FOOTBALL

FRANKIE SAVES CHRISTMAS

FRANK LAMPARD

LITTLE, BROWN BOOKS FOR YOUNG READERS
www.lbkids.co.uk

LITTLE, BROWN BOOKS FOR YOUNG READERS

First published in Great Britain in 2014 by Little, Brown Books
for Young Readers

1 3 5 7 9 10 8 6 4 2

A CIP catalogue record for this book is
available from the British Library.

ISBN 978-1-5102-0103-3

Typeset in Cantarell by M Rules
Printed and bound in Great Britain by
Clays Ltd, St Ives plc

Papers used by LBYR are from well-managed forests
and other responsible sources.

MIX
Paper from
responsible sources
FSC® C104740

Little, Brown Books for Young Readers
An imprint of
Little, Brown Book Group
100 Victoria Embankment
London EC4Y 0DY

An Hachette UK Company
www.hachette.co.uk

www.lbkids.co.uk

To my mum Pat, who encouraged me to do my homework in between kicking a ball all around the house, and is still with me every step of the way.

*Welcome to a fantastic
Fantasy League – the greatest
football competition ever held
in this world or any other!*

*You'll need four on a team,
so choose carefully. This is a lot
more serious than a game in the
park. You'll never know who your
next opponents will be, or
where you'll face them.*

*So lace up your boots, players,
and good luck! The whistle's
about to blow!*

The Ref

PART ONE

CHAPTER 1

Frankie chewed on the end of
his pencil, leaning over his letter
to Santa. It was the day before
Christmas Eve, and he was having a
sleepover with his friends, Charlie
and Louise. They sat beside each
other at the table in the living
room, writing their Christmas lists.

His mum and dad were watching TV. They had a fire roaring in the hearth, and the glow of the flames reflected in the baubles hanging from the Christmas tree. Frankie loved this time of year.

"This is hard!" he said to Charlie and Louise. "What have you guys written?"

Charlie turned his piece of paper around, but all Frankie could see was an untidy scrawl. "What does that say?" he asked.

"New goalie gloves," said Charlie. He was wearing his old ones and held up his hands. "See — these are really worn out."

"That's because you never take
them off," said Louise.

"A good keeper is always ready,"
Charlie told her, grinning.

"Maybe," said Frankie, "but
I hope Santa can read your
handwriting!"

Frankie had an idea and returned
to his own list. He wrote:

Football boots, please (size 13,
red if possible)

Max was lying on the rug in front of
the fire and whined softly.

Frankie added something else to
his list:

Bone for Max

Louise was frowning. "I don't know
why I bother," she said. "I asked for
a new football kit last year, and I
got a yellow dress!"

"What have you written this
year?" said Charlie.

Louise showed them:

A new football kit (not a dress)

"Hey, losers," said Kevin, barging through the door from the kitchen.

"Found my football yet?" asked Frankie.

Kevin lowered his glance. "I told you — I haven't touched it."

"Quiet, you two," said Frankie's dad.

Frankie always knew when his brother was lying because he couldn't meet his eye. The ball had gone missing from his wardrobe a couple of days before. He leant over the table and whispered so his

9

parents wouldn't hear. "You know it can be trouble, Kev. Seriously, where is it?"

Kevin shrugged. Then he caught sight of their lists and rolled his eyes. "Santa isn't real."

"Leave them alone, Kev," Frankie's mum called over.

"Santa's for little kids," Kevin grumbled. "I mean – how are you supposed to even get these letters to him? The last Christmas post went two days ago."

Frankie realised he was right. Charlie and Louise looked worried too.

"Tell you what," said Kevin. "Let's

use Santa's *special* postal service. He comes down the chimney, so that's how we'll send him the lists." Before Frankie could stop him, he lunged and grabbed all their pieces of paper. Then he screwed them up, pulled back the fire guard and tossed the balls of paper into the fire.

"No!" cried Frankie. He watched the papers blacken and burn to nothing. He turned towards his brother, then spotted that their dad was watching them.

"What's going on?" he said.

Frankie pointed to the fire. "Kev burned our Christmas lists."

"Tell-tale!" said Kevin.

"That wasn't nice," said Frankie's dad, shaking his head. "Go to your room, Kevin."

As his brother stalked off, Frankie watched helplessly as smoke drifted up the chimney.

"Santa is real, isn't he, Dad?" said Frankie.

"Of course he is," his dad replied. "Remember that mince pie we left out last year? *Someone* ate it."

"That was you!" Kevin called down the stairs.

His dad shrugged. "It wasn't, actually. And besides, you were tucked up in bed. How would you know?"

They could all hear Kevin snorting with disbelief from upstairs, but his dad gave Frankie a wink. "Why don't you write your lists again on the computer? We'll email them to Santa."

Frankie grinned. "Has Santa got an email address?"

"Of course he has," said Frankie's dad. "Even Father Christmas has to move with the times."

Later that night they were all in Frankie's room. Charlie and Louise were asleep on blow-up beds on the floor beside Frankie's bed. Charlie was wearing pyjamas covered in pictures of rockets and spacecraft. His gloves were still on his hands, resting on top of the quilt. Louise's sleeping bag came right up to the tip of her nose, covering most of her ears. She'd said it was the only way to avoid Charlie's snoring.

Frankie couldn't sleep. If Kevin was hiding his magic football, they could be in deep trouble. The football opened portals to other worlds, and in the wrong hands – *Kevin's* hands – he dreaded to think what mischief it could cause.

But he could hardly tell his parents – they'd never believe him. Frankie decided that the next morning, he and his friends would do a thorough search of the house, from top to bottom.

The football has to be somewhere, he told himself.

He turned over, pulling his duvet tighter, when he heard a noise.

It sounded like a tapping, coming from somewhere near the window. Frankie sat up in bed, and pulled open the curtains a tiny bit. It was a clear night, with the moon shining full and bright over the garden below.

A shaft of moonlight fell across the room, and Charlie and Louise both stirred.

"Is it morning?" mumbled Charlie.

"No," whispered Frankie. "I thought I heard a noise, that's all."

Louise peered from the sleeping bag, pushing her messy hair out of her eyes. "You were probably dreaming. Close that curtain, will you?"

Frankie was about to do as she said, when he heard the sound once more. This time, though, it was louder. *Knock knock knock.*

It was definitely coming from

somewhere nearby. Then Frankie
noticed something very strange
indeed. His Christmas snow globe
sat on the windowsill and in the
moonlight he could see that tiny
flakes of fake snow were whirling
around, even though he hadn't
touched the globe. Usually, he
had to give the globe a really
good shake to stir up the snow.
"Look at this!" he said to the
others.

Louise and Charlie scrambled
up on to his bed, and peered at the
snow globe. Inside was a model
castle. But, as well as the snow,
something else was moving.

Frankie's heart raced as a tiny figure dressed in green emerged from the snowy scene and knocked on the inside of the globe. He waved his arms wildly.

"He's trying to tell us something," said Louise. "What is it?"

A coating of mist was forming on the inside of the globe. The figure removed a white glove and used a fingertip to scrawl something in the mist. He wrote in large letters. Frankie and his friends watched, holding their breath as a message began to take form. *O U . . .*

"OUTSIDE!" Louise cried.

"He must be very clever," Frankie said. "He was writing that back to front for us to be able to read it on the other side of the glass." The little figure was pulling his glove back on. Then he pointed urgently at the window.

Frankie looked at his friends. "You read what he's telling us. Let's go outside!"

"Now?" said Charlie, giving a shiver.

Frankie jumped off the bed and pulled on his jumper.

"We can wrap up warm," he told his friends. "Come on. How often do we have miniature people giving us messages from inside snow globes? This must be important!"

Charlie and Louise looked at each other and gave a nod. Then they raced to pull their clothes on over their pyjamas. Frankie opened his bedroom door with a creak and peered out. His brother's door was slightly open, but it was dark inside. The last thing they needed was to wake Kev.

Frankie put his fingers to his lips and edged out towards the stairs. The others tiptoed after him. Frankie crept down the stairs, avoiding the fourth from the bottom, which he knew creaked badly. Louise and Charlie followed his signals and did the same.

Max was still basking beside the embers of the fire, but stirred as they approached.

By the back door, Frankie handed Charlie and Louise scarves and hats from the coat-rail, and they all found their shoes. Then Frankie eased open the door.

The garden was silent and empty. They stood together in a huddle, their breath making clouds in the air. The grass sparkled with frost.

Max's ears pricked up, and he arched his neck to the sky. Frankie saw a movement among the stars.

At first he thought it must be a comet, trailing glittering sparks like falling stars. The shape came closer and closer. Frankie narrowed his eyes and spotted . . . animals! They were hauling a wooden sled the size of a car. The creatures had dappled coats and small bushy white tails. And they seemed to be wearing some sort of pointy hats.

No, not hats . . . antlers.

"They're reindeer!" gasped Louise.

The sled swooped over the nearby houses on Frankie's street, then dipped out of sight for a moment. "It's going to crash into number sixty-four!" said Frankie.

But at the last moment the sled climbed again, just clearing the garden fence and leaning to one side.

"Their formation's all wrong," said Charlie.

The front two reindeer landed, hooves thumping into the grass and bells jangling around their necks. The rest hit the ground behind them and the sled slid across the lawn towards Frankie and his friends.

"Look out!" he said, leaping back.

The reindeer cantered past and the sled eventually stopped just a few metres short of the ornamental pond. Frankie was a little disappointed not to see Santa holding the reins. In fact, no one seemed to be driving at all.

No wonder they're struggling to fly straight, thought Frankie.

Louise and Charlie were wide-eyed and Frankie realised he was holding his breath. He let it out in a rush. It wasn't as if they'd even been playing with the football, so what was a magic sled doing in his garden?

"What now?" said Charlie.

"You climb aboard, silly," said a voice. It came from the lead reindeer, twitching his antlers.

"Did you just speak?" Louise asked, open-mouthed.

The reindeer wiggled his tail. "Of course! Come on. Mr Claus needs your help."

CHAPTER 2

"Are you Rudolph?" asked Charlie.

"Rudolph?" repeated the reindeer, looking around at his friends. All the other animals laughed. "Rudolph retired *years* ago. I'm Pelé. And these are my friends Ronaldo, Zidane, Crespo, Lineker, Cantona and Cruyff."

Frankie counted. "How come there are only seven of you? Doesn't Santa have eight reindeer? And aren't you meant to be called names like Donner and Blitzen?"

"Long story," said Pelé. "No time to tell you now."

"Erm . . . could you ask Zidane to stop chewing on the roses, please?" said Frankie.

The reindeer lifted its head. "I was just sniffing them," it said, petals falling from its lips.

"Are you coming?" said Pelé. "We only have a few hours left to save Christmas."

"Us?" said Louise.

"That's right," said Pelé. "Who better to help than the ones who have the magic football? Santa's heard how great you are in a crisis."

"But I *don't* have the football," said Frankie. "I haven't seen it for days."

"Well, something brought us to your house," said Pelé. "It doesn't really matter. Can you help us or not?"

Frankie glanced at his friends. Both Charlie and Louise nodded. Max jumped on to the sled, settling himself on a red velvet cushion.

"I guess that settles it," Frankie said. He hopped over the side as well and his friends climbed on board after him.

"Kick-off time!" said Pelé.

The sled moved slowly at first as the reindeer heaved in their harnesses, but then it picked up speed as they travelled down the length of the lawn. Frankie winced when he saw the deep gouges in the pristine grass – his dad would go bananas. Pelé's hooves left the ground first and the others followed, hooves churning in the air. Last of all, the sled's nose lifted, and suddenly they were airborne, shooting over the houses, rising higher and higher.

"So what's the problem with Christmas?" Frankie yelled to the nearest reindeer.

It didn't seem to hear him over the rush of wind.

"Better just enjoy the ride," said Max. He was sitting up, tongue lolling in the night air.

"You can talk again!" said Frankie. Whenever they entered a magical world, Max could make himself understood. *This must mean that the football's magic is still working*, Frankie thought. *Even if I don't know where it is.*

"Yes, I can!" said Max, "and I've got an admission to make — I'm the one who ate that mince pie last year!"

Frankie laughed and settled back to watch the world whizz by below.

It was hard to tell how much time passed as they shot through the clouds. Frankie checked his watch, but it seemed to have stopped at midnight; the hands were still. "Hey, look!" he showed his watch to Louise. She glanced at her wrist then showed her watch to Frankie. The same thing had happened to hers!

From time to time, when the clouds broke, Frankie saw snatches of sea below — endless, rolling dark waves — then fields and mountains. The bells around the necks of the reindeer rang out as they led the sled on under the star-filled sky.

"I wonder where we're going," said Charlie, shivering.

"That's the North Star, straight ahead," said Louise, pointing at a particularly bright dot in the sky. Her dad had a telescope, she'd told Frankie once, so she knew all about the night sky. "I think we are heading towards the Arctic Circle."

Frankie knew he should have

felt much colder than he did, but a strange tingling across his body kept him warm. Finally, the reindeer dipped their heads and flew the sled down to ground. Frankie gasped as they broke through the clouds.

Below, there was white snow as far as he could see. Now and again, the stretches of snow would be broken up by patches of fir trees. They descended lower and lower, following the gentle slopes and valleys. Louise's arm shot forward. "Wow – look at that!" she cried, pointing.

Frankie saw a tall castle built of

lilac stone, with domes and spires, rising from the ground ahead. It was a lot like the one in his snow globe.

"Welcome to Santa's palace," said the reindeer at the back. He wore a collar saying "Lineker, G".

The sled landed in front of the building, gliding gently to a halt. As Frankie and the others hopped off on to hard-packed snow, a small boy dressed in green came running through the gates of the palace, rubbing his hands together. When he got closer, Frankie saw he was actually a man, but only about three feet tall. His ears were long and pointed.

"About time!" he cried. "The boss
has been waiting for you lot. Quick,
come inside."

He turned and rushed back
indoors. Frankie shrugged to his
friends and they followed the little
man.

"Is he . . . an elf?" muttered
Charlie.

"No, I'm a tiny Vulcan," said the man. "Only joking. Of course I'm an elf. Name's Robin. Pleased to meet you."

Inside the grand oak doors of the palace was a large entrance hall lit with torches on the walls. The room was warm from the flames. Sweeping steps led to an upper level, and corridors stretched off in all directions. More elves scurried back and forth, loaded down with wrapped presents.

Max watched one of the elves race past with a bone-shaped parcel. "Do you think that's for me?" he asked hopefully.

"Shhh," Frankie told him, as Robin gave their dog a strange look.

"It's always busy at this time of year," said the elf, turning back to the others. "This way, please." He veered off down a set of stairs, sliding along the banister. Frankie had to run to keep up.

At the bottom, they found themselves in a huge room. It had a conveyor belt running through it. Frankie watched the presents moving around the room — hundreds of them, in every shape and size, all in different wrapping paper. Huge sacks lay at intervals along the floor, and more elves were taking presents off the belt to place them inside.

In the centre of the room stood a man holding a clipboard. He wore a tracksuit decorated with holly leaves and his cheeks gleamed red over his bushy white beard.

"They're here, boss!" called Robin.

Boss? thought Frankie. *Surely that can't be . . .*

"Santa Claus?" said Charlie aloud.

The man spotted them and his eyebrows shot up. "At last! Thank goodness you could come," he said, tossing the clipboard aside. "That's

right, I'm Santa Claus. Father Christmas. Old Saint Nick. Call me what you will."

"You're a lot less round than you look on all the cards," said Max, trotting around the man.

"It's all the running around," said Santa, patting his taut stomach. "By December 26th, with all those mince pies, it will be a different matter."

"Boss," interrupted Robin, "maybe you should explain why we have dragged them to Lapland?"

Frankie, Louise and Charlie all looked at each other. "So, that's where we are!" Frankie said. Their

past two adventures had taken
them to Brazil, China . . . and now
they were in Lapland.

"Yes, right," said Santa. "We have
a problem. This room sorts all the
presents into different categories.
Dolls, computer games, clothes,
and so on. Well, one sack has gone
missing – the one with the football
presents! At first we thought they'd
been lost in the chaos." He waved
a hand at the looping belts criss-
crossing the room. "But we found
this!" He fished in his pocket and
held up a lock of thick white hair.

Frankie frowned, and looked at
his friends. "What is it?"

Santa lowered his voice. "I'd recognise this hair anywhere. It comes from the coat of the Krampus!"

"Pardon?" said Charlie.

Louise stepped forward. "The Krampus is a myth from folklore," she said. "A creature who punishes naughty children at Christmas time."

Frankie and Charlie stared at her. "How do you know about that?" asked Charlie.

Louise shrugged. "I've been reading our encyclopaedia at home."

"Sadly, he is no myth,"

interrupted Santa. "He's real, with a very bad temper. Robin — the footage, please."

The small elf ran off.

"So, this Krampus stole the presents?" said Frankie. "That's horrible!"

Santa sighed. "We haven't seen him for many years, but it seems now he has struck again. Unfortunately for him, he sheds hair everywhere, so it's always very easy to tell when he's paid us a visit. Ah, here's Robin."

The elf had picked up Santa's clipboard. Up close, Frankie saw it was actually a computer tablet.

Santa turned it towards them and hit the play button on the screen. An image came up of the packing room where they stood now. Lots of round, bouncy presents were falling off the end of a belt into a sack. Suddenly a reindeer crept into the shot, accompanied by a tall, hunched figure in a hood. The person gave a low, mean laugh, then hitched the sack of presents to the reindeer's harness. Together, they dragged it away. Wisps of white hair fell to the floor behind them.

"Who's the reindeer?" asked Frankie.

"Maradona," said Santa, with a

sigh. "He's turned bad and gone to work for the Krampus."

"So that's why there are only seven reindeer," said Frankie.

"What I can't work out," said Robin, "is who opened the door to let them in."

Santa tossed the tablet aside, and Robin dived to catch it. "That doesn't matter right now. I need a team to search for the presents. A football team, quick enough to rescue the football presents. I can't think of anyone better than you!"

"Why can't you go?" asked Charlie.

"No time!" said Santa. His

shoulders sagged. "There's too much to do here. If you can't help me, I don't know what I'll do."

Frankie took a deep breath. *We can't let innocent children miss out on their football presents. They'll start to think that Santa doesn't exist!*

"Okay. Where do we look for the Krampus?" he asked.

Santa clapped his hands together. "Thank you! Take a team of dogs and a sled and head east. That's where his ice-cave lair used to be."

"I could go with them," said Robin.

Santa frowned. "I'm not sure, Robin. I need my most trusted elf here."

Frankie noticed some of the other elves share a glance.

"But what if they get lost?" said Robin, pacing back and forth.

Santa hesitated for a moment, then nodded. "All right. Off you go."

"Yes, boss," said Robin, turning on his heel and marching away. "Follow me!"

As Frankie and his friends hurried away, Santa called after them. "Be careful. The Krampus won't make it easy for you. He keeps bad company. He used to hang around with an abominable snowman."

"You mean a yeti?" asked Louise.

"No," said Santa, "just a very unpleasant snowman. Good luck!"

CHAPTER 3

Robin led them from the back of
the palace to a stable. As they
approached, Frankie could hear
howling and barking. Max gave a
low growl. When Robin opened the
double doors, a team of dogs leapt
out, tugging a wooden sled behind
them. Frankie jerked back, and

Max jumped up into his arms, but the dogs stopped in front of them, wagging their tails. They had thick coats of pale fur and bright blue eyes.

"Hop on," said Robin, grasping the reins and jumping on to the back of the sled. Frankie and his friends had to stand on the cross-pieces of the sled in front of him, just a fraction off the ground. As soon as they were on board, the dogs strained.

"Go!" Robin cried, then gave a sharp whistle. The sled lurched off into the snow, kicking up slush as the dogs barked with excitement.

Max ducked beneath Robin's platform and pulled out a red woolly hat with his teeth. It was the perfect size for a little dog and Frankie helped him put it on.

"There you go, boy," he said.

Robin took out a compass. He steered the animals with just the lightest tug on the leather reins. Soon the palace was lost behind

the trees. Frankie squinted into the white glare ahead. In the distance were huge mountains, completely covered in snow.

"It's beautiful," said Charlie, over the swish of the sled's runners.

They passed bristling trees and small wooden huts, which he guessed must be the elves' homes. It was hard to imagine anything living here, but he saw the occasional bird flapping from a snowy branch, or a light-footed hare darting between the trees.

The huskies ran and ran, their legs pumping, pink tongues lolling. Frankie spotted something up ahead – the ground looked a slightly different colour, almost blue, and seemed to dip away.

"Slow down!" he said to Robin.

But the elf flicked the reins harder. "We need to keep moving. It's a long way to the—"

Suddenly, the ground creaked under the sled's runners as a crack in the snow's crust zig-zagged towards them. It was coming from the direction of the strange dip ahead. Frankie grabbed a rein and yanked it hard. The sled veered left, almost toppling over. Charlie crashed into Louise and they both fell out into the snow.

"Hey!" said Robin, straightening his hat. "Why did you do that?"

Frankie nodded to the path they'd been following. "Because of that!" he said.

Just a few metres further on, the ground had split apart in a crevasse. Frankie stepped off the sled and walked carefully to the edge. He peered over and gasped. He couldn't even see the bottom.

The others joined him. "Good work, Frankie," said Charlie. "That was a close shave!"

Robin stayed well back from the edge. "We'll have to turn back," he announced.

"And let the Krampus win?" said Louise. "No way!"

Robin folded his arms. "We'll have to go back empty-handed," he said. "It's too far to jump." Frankie stared at him. Why was he giving up so easily?

"Maybe not," said Frankie. He pointed to the huskies. "If we get a good run-up, we might make it. Help me build a ramp of snow on this side."

"Great idea!" said Charlie. "We can jump it like we do on our bikes down at the park."

Frankie pushed snow towards the lip of the crevasse, then

stamped it down. The others began to help – even Robin – and it wasn't long before they'd packed the snow into a wedge shape, climbing towards the edge of the drop.

Frankie boarded the sled again, but Robin stayed on the snow. "Are you coming with us?" asked Frankie.

The elf looked uncertain, but finally he jumped on as well. "I must be mad," he grumbled.

Frankie steered the sled well back from the edge, then turned it round.

"Hold on tight!" he said, lifting the reins. The huskies barked wildly.

"Wait!" said Max. He jumped off the sled and grabbed one of the loose straps in his teeth, ready to help.

Frankie was proud of his little dog. "Go!" he cried.

The sled launched forward as the dogs pulled as one, feet kicking up loose snow. The wooden platform shook as they rocketed towards the gap. Frankie's knuckles were white and the icy breeze whipped his face.

"We're going to make it," he muttered to himself. "We *have* to make it."

But the crevasse looked wider by the second.

The first team of huskies reached the end of the ramp, and leapt into the air. Frankie felt suddenly weightless as the dogs launched into empty space, paws tucked under their bodies. They were soaring through the air!

CHAPTER 4

SLAM!

The sled's runners hit solid ground and Frankie looked back to see the rear landing just over the gap.

"We made it!" he shouted.

Louise patted him on the back and Max leapt out from the other dogs and back on to the sled, wagging his tail. "It was the extra muscle that did it," Max said. "Not sure how we'll get back, though."

"Let's worry about that later," said Frankie.

Robin was cowering in the bottom of the sled with his hands over his eyes. "Are we still alive?" he asked in a shaky voice.

"Yes," said Charlie. "Now, which way?"

The elf stood. "Let's take a short cut," he said, nodding ahead. He took up position at the back of the sled again.

They set off at speed. Robin guided the huskies skilfully around a clump of boulders towards a passage threading between two groups of firs.

Louise leant close to Frankie's ear. "I'm not sure about this route," she said. "Santa said we had to go east, but from the moon's position, I think we're going south."

"Robin said this was a shortcut," said Frankie.

"Er . . . where's he gone?" said Max.

Frankie and Louise turned round and saw that the elf had vanished from the back of the sled, where he'd been standing just a moment before. No one was driving the sled, and the huskies were hurtling headlong through the valley bottom.

The sled shook and rocked as it flew over the uneven snow, and Frankie struggled to grab hold of the reins. When he had them, he tugged hard and the huskies came to a gradual stop, panting.

"He must have fallen off," said Charlie. "I hope he's okay."

Heart thumping, Frankie's eyes followed their trail backwards until they spotted a green shape. It was Robin, but he looked absolutely fine. He was looking up one of the slopes, then brought his fingers to his lips and let out a shrill whistle.

"What's he doing?" asked Louise.

"I don't like this at all," said Charlie.

Frankie's eyes scanned the slope and at the top he spotted something else. A horse? No, it had antlers – it was a reindeer. The creature was stomping the snow, right above where their sled had stopped. Something about the shape of his antlers was familiar. He remembered the footage Santa had shown them.

"It's Maradona!" he said. "The rogue reindeer."

A low rumble like distant thunder

sounded, and part of the slope
seemed to shift. Frankie's blood ran
cold. Cracks appeared across the
perfect snow and the whole slope
began to slough off. The thunder
became louder.

"Avalanche!" Frankie yelled.

Maradona was using his hooves
to cause a massive snowfall!

Snow crashed down the valley's sides towards them, ripping trees from the ground.

Frankie jumped from the sled and quickly unfastened the huskies. "Go! Get away!" he shouted. The dogs sprinted, lightning fast. There was no way Frankie and his friends could run that fast. They were trapped.

"Turn over the sled!" cried Louise. "We can shelter behind it."

The snow roared towards them. Frankie and his friends gripped the edge of the sled and tried to heave it over. Frankie's arms strained and he gritted his teeth. With a roar of effort, they pulled the sled over and threw themselves behind it, Max scampering between Frankie's ankles, just as the first blast of snow hit them.

The avalanche crashed over the sled, carrying bits of trees and rocks with it. Frankie saw his friends' faces twisted with fear as they sheltered.

An eerie silence fell, broken only by the sound of their heavy breathing and the weird creaking as the snow settled around them. They were in a pocket of air, almost like a prison cell. Most of the snow had gone right over them, but Frankie's head and shoulders were covered. There was a small gap of sky above. "Is everyone all right?" he asked.

His friends nodded, and together they picked their way out, climbing over the rugged snow.

Frankie looked up at the slope above, but the reindeer had gone.

"Maradona must have been on the lookout," he said. "And it looks like Robin was working with him all along — he led us right into a trap, then whistled to his accomplice to start the avalanche."

Louise nodded. "Santa Claus wondered how the Krampus got in

to steal the presents — now we have our answer. A treacherous elf!"

"So what do we do?" said Charlie.

"Keep going," said Frankie. "If the rogue reindeer was waiting for us, we must be close to the ice caves where the Krampus lives."

They trudged further down the valley, and sure enough at the bottom, they saw several dark openings in the hill ahead. "We're here," he said. Frankie led the way over the snow, eyes peeled. What if the Krampus was watching them already?

He was about twenty metres

from one of the cave mouths when Louise shoved him hard in the back. "Duck!" she yelled. Frankie fell to his knees in the snow as something splatted right in his face.

Snowballs!

CHAPTER 5

"Oof!" cried Louise, as one hit her shoulder and spun her round.

"They're coming from the cave!" said Max, as he skipped to dodge another.

A huge shape emerged from the shadow of the cave mouth — two spheres balanced on top of each other with spindly branches for arms, and a jutting carrot for a nose. He wore a green and red scarf and a top hat that cast his face in shadow. *It can't be . . .*

"I guess *that's* the abominable snowman," barked Max.

"No trespassers!" roared the snowman.

It grabbed another two handfuls of snow from its side and hurled them faster than a baseball player. Charlie leapt in front of Frankie and caught them both.

"You'll never get past me!" he shouted.

The snowman's eyes glinted

darkly. "See if you can stop this," he boomed.

A snowball seemed to grow by magic from the ground in front of him, but this one was as big as a football. Charlie's eyes widened, but he stood firm, spreading his arms. "Charlie, don't!" said Louise.

Too late. The snow boulder

hurtled towards him, striking him right in the chest and sending him flying. Charlie slid across the ground and landed in a heap, groaning. Frankie ran to his friend, and with Louise's help, dragged him behind a tree. Charlie's eyelids were flickering.

"Are you okay?" said Louise.

His lips moved a little and his eyes opened, unfocused. "Did I save it?" he mumbled.

"You did," said Louise. "But that was risky, Charlie — he could have killed you!"

Frankie glanced out from behind the tree, and snow

exploded over his head as another giant snowball hit the trunk above. The snowman was standing in the shadow of the cave mouth. While he was there, they couldn't get near. The sun had risen higher in the sky, and its rays bathed Frankie's face.

"That's the key!" said Frankie. "We need to lure him out into the sun. The heat will make him melt. Then we can get to the Krampus and find the presents!"

Louise smiled. "Okay, captain, so how do we get the snowman to come out?"

Frankie swelled his chest. "We

have to give him a target he can't refuse."

"You're not thinking . . .?" Louise began.

Frankie jumped out from their hiding place and ran towards the caves. Straight away the missiles started flying, whooshing past his ears. Frankie tried to imagine he was back on the football pitch, running with the ball from his own half, dodging tackles and making runs. He feinted left and darted right, he changed his speed and body positions.

"Over here, Mr Freeze!" called Max.

Frankie risked a look back and saw that both his friends had emerged into the open too.

The snowman's arms were a blur, and he grunted and hissed in anger as his snowballs missed their target. Frankie saw him shifting further out from the shadows. But as soon as a cloud passed from in front of the sun, the snowman scrambled back into the shadows of the cave.

He's scared of the sun, thought Frankie. *I have to try harder.*

Frankie pretended to slip and fell to the ground with a cry. He'd never take a dive when playing for real, but he'd seen others do it and fool the referee. He lay on his back on the cold snow, hoping the snowman was convinced.

Footsteps crunched through the snow and a shadow fell over him.

The snowman looked even taller close up. Water droplets poured off his head, collecting in a puddle at his feet. His face was turning slushy.

"The Krampu*sh* told me *Sh*anta would *sh*end *sh*omeone," said the snowman, his voice slurring as he melted. Then he stooped and gathered a huge boulder of snow in his arms, lifting it over his head.

He's going to crush me! thought Frankie, throwing his arms up to defend himself. *I won't be able to save Christmas after all!*

PART TWO

CHAPTER 6

Frankie heard two thuds and looked up to see the snowman staggering backwards. He'd been hit! One snowball had knocked his carrot nose sideways, the other had smashed into the middle of his chest. He dropped the giant snowball as more rained down on him.

"Get away from our friend!" yelled Louise.

She and Charlie were advancing, scooping up snow and hurling it at the snowman. Snowballs hit his body and head, and he didn't have time to fight back. Frankie recognised the determined look in Louise's eyes from the football pitch. She was pushing for the counter attack! One snowball landed right over the snowman's left eye. He flailed and roared, spinning around.

"That's it!" said Frankie. "Cover his other eye too!"

He joined in the attack, aiming

at the snowman's head. Soon the other eye was covered as well and the snowman stumbled blindly through the sun–bathed snow. He was melting quickly now, sinking to the ground.

"I'll get you!" he cried, swinging stodgily around as his body vanished in the sunlight, like a man sinking in quicksand. "Come back here!"

But he was still shrinking, and only his top half remained. One after the other, his stick arms fell off. Soon the snowman was just a hump of snow, topped with a hat and a green and red striped scarf.

"Thanks, guys!" said Frankie.

"No problem," said Charlie, patting his gloves together to shake off the loose snow.

Louise was already striding for the cave mouth. "Let's go and find these presents," she said.

Max sniffed at the carrot, then followed, and Frankie and Charlie went after him.

As Frankie walked slowly beside his friends, his eyes began to adjust to the dim light. Then he saw figures ahead and his breath caught in his chest. He stopped. The figures stopped too.

"Hello?" said Frankie.

His voice echoed back.

"Who are they?" whispered Charlie.

Frankie took another step, and the figures did the same. He noticed they had a small dog with them as well.

Suddenly it became clear. He lifted his arm. The figure ahead did the same.

"It's just our reflections!" he cried.

Frankie ran his hands over a smooth sheet of ice, polished like a mirror.

"Weird," said Louise. "How did this get down here?"

"There are more!" said Max.

He had trotted a few metres further, and stood in front of another ice-sheet, wagging his tail.

"And over there!" said Charlie, pointing the other way. Frankie walked on in wonder through the cavern. There were hundreds of ice-sheets that had formed along the walls, all at different angles. He could see himself from every angle and it made him dizzy.

"We have to stay focused," he said. "This is probably some sort of trap."

They followed the tunnel between the ice-mirrors. It was like walking among a huge crowd, even though there were only four of them.

Then Frankie saw another movement – a dark shape flitting across the mirrors – and spun around.

"What was that?" he hissed.

"I didn't see anything," said Charlie.

Frankie froze. "That . . ." he said. Two long, curved horns were rising up behind them, reflected in the mirrors. Beneath the horns appeared a long head, covered in hair.

They all swivelled around, but were too late. Whatever it was had disappeared again.

"What do we have here?" cackled a voice. "A bunch of *children*?"

"Who are you?" said Frankie, eyes scanning the cavern.

"Who am I?" said the voice, becoming more high-pitched. "Who *am* I? I am the Krampus!"

He stepped out from behind an ice-mirror. He looked like some sort of goat-man. Even though he stood on two legs, his feet were cloven hooves, and his body was covered in grubby long hair. His sickly green eyes glittered.

"What are you doing here, little ones?" he asked.

"We've come to get back the presents you stole," Louise said.

The Krampus chuckled. "Is that right? I suppose *he* sent you?"

"Santa Claus, you mean," said Charlie.

The Krampus covered both his ears. "Don't say his horrible name to me," he screeched. "I *hate* that fiend!"

"How can you hate Santa?" said Frankie. "He brings happiness to people all over the world."

"Not this year," snapped the Krampus. "There are going to be some very unhappy children crying by their Christmas trees!"

CHAPTER 7

"You're nothing but a thief," said Louise. "Where are the presents?"

"You'll never find them," said the Krampus. "I'll play football all year round with the balls I stole. Each kick will be sweet, thinking of the Christmases I've ruined."

"We'll stop you," said Frankie.

"No, you won't," said the Krampus. "You'll wander through my ice maze until you freeze!"

The Krampus pranced away around a bend, and Frankie ran after him. But as he rounded the corner he saw lots of versions of his enemy, all running away. He sprinted after one.

BANG!

Frankie ran straight into his own reflection, leaving a splintered crack across the mirror.

"Are you okay?" said Louise, arriving at his side.

Frankie rubbed his head, and stared around him. The Krampus

had vanished. "I'm fine, but where did he go?"

"Over there!" said Charlie, pointing.

Frankie saw the Krampus hiding, but he spun out of sight again, appearing to Frankie's left. He darted that way, but then realised it was just a reflection. Everywhere he looked, there was a version of their foe, and of themselves.

"You'll never find me," said the Krampus. "Only I know the cave's secret paths."

It was impossible to work out where his voice was coming from. Frankie walked one way, then the other. His head began to spin and his eyes hurt. He felt like he was playing a team of a hundred opponents, and they were running rings around him. He could still see Max and the others, but he wasn't sure if it was really them any longer, or just their reflections.

"You'll all go mad in here," said

the Krampus by his ear. What if the Krampus was right? What if this was a game they simply couldn't win?

"I can smell him," said Max. "He seems to be everywhere. It's probably all that stinky hair falling off him."

"Dogs are *really* stupid," said the Krampus. "Goodbye, foolish children!"

Frankie heard his cloven footsteps clattering away and fought to control the panic in his chest. *If we don't stay calm now, we're done for.*

"What do we do?" asked Louise with a tremor in her voice.

Frankie realised they were all

scared. He needed to be strong — a real captain came up with a game plan.

The ice maze was like a prison. *So how do we break out?*

His foot knocked into a rock on the floor, and an idea sprang into his head.

"Smash the ice," he said.

"Pardon?" said Charlie.

Frankie picked up the rock. "Find a stone, and throw it at the ice-sheets," he said. "If we destroy the mirrors, we'll be able to see more clearly where we are."

He drew back his hand and flung his rock at the nearest one. It splintered and cracked, the pieces falling to the ground.

"Good thinking!" said Louise. Max scampered back and forth as the three of them went from mirror to mirror, shattering each. Frankie was breathing heavily by the time they'd finished and they stood together in the centre of the cavern. Without all the mirrors, it didn't seem that big. There were several narrow doorways in the rocky walls, all leading off in different directions. Max lowered his nose to the ground, rushing between them. He stopped at one. "I think he went down here!" he barked.

"We're coming to find you, Krampus!" shouted Frankie.

"I'm waiting for you!" came the reply.

Frankie steeled his nerves as he led the others into the tunnel. *We got past a crevasse, an avalanche and a murderous snowman. We're not going to stop now!*

They followed a tunnel, sometimes having to stoop low to avoid banging their heads.

"Are you sure this is the way?" asked Charlie.

Max padded along at Frankie's feet. "Oh yes — his scent is getting stronger all the time."

The tunnel opened up ahead, and Frankie slowed. They emerged into a huge cave glowing with blue light from below. The ground was covered with a lake of pristine ice. At the far end stood two tree trunks with their branches chopped off, like football posts. The Krampus was leaning against one of them, wearing a football kit that was far too small. The whole place smelled like a stable that hadn't been cleaned for a long time.

"You'll pay for destroying my ice maze," he sneered.

"Hey, that football strip is just

like the one I want for Christmas," said Louise.

The Krampus laughed. "Correction, little lady. This *is* the football strip you want for Christmas." He gestured behind him, and Frankie saw a huge sack of presents spilling on to the ground. "I do enjoy unwrapping gifts addressed to other people."

"The game's up," said Frankie. "Hand over the presents."

The Krampus picked up a round present and tore off the wrapping paper to reveal a brand new football.

"The game is only just beginning," he said.

CHAPTER 8

"I bet you don't even like football,"
said Charlie.

The Krampus spun the ball on
his finger. "I'm the best goalkeeper
in Lapland, actually. Even the elf
first team couldn't score past me. If
you'd seen my penalty save . . ."

"Prove it," said Frankie. "Play us.

If we can score a goal, you give us back the presents."

The Krampus hesitated, frowning. He cast a tiny glance behind himself, and for a brief moment Frankie thought he saw other figures in the shadows. He couldn't be sure.

"He's scared," said Louise. "He's all talk."

"Silence!" said the Krampus. "You have a deal, children. If you score past me between these trees, you take the presents." A cruel smile spread over his hairy face. "But if you lose . . ."

"Yes?" said Frankie.

"If you lose, I'll tether you to my sled and you can pull me round for a whole year."

Frankie looked to his friends. Charlie's jaw was tight, his face pale.

"Now who's scared?" said the Krampus with a nasty grin. "I take it you won't accept my deal? Oh well, lots of children will have a miserable Christmas . . ."

Charlie nodded to Frankie.

"I'll look forward to beating him," muttered Louise.

"No one ruins Christmas!" added Max.

Frankie turned from his friends,

hope surging through him. "We'll take you on, Krampus," he said.

"Excellent," said their foe. He grabbed another present and read the label aloud *"Merry Xmas Charles, from Santa."* He looked at Charlie as he ripped open the paper and pulled out a pair of goalie gloves. "Ah, just what I need!"

"Don't worry, Charlie," said Frankie, seeing the anger on his friend's face. "We'll get them back."

The Krampus kicked the football across the ice, and it skidded right to where Frankie and his friends stood at the edge. "Let's play!" he said.

This shouldn't be too hard, thought Frankie. *Four against one.*

He jumped down on to the ice, and straight away felt it give at his feet with a loud crack. Splits appeared across the surface in all directions.

"Oh, I forgot to mention the ice is quite thin," said the Krampus, standing between the posts.

"Quick! Into positions!" called Frankie to his team. "Before it breaks up."

Louise, Charlie and Max climbed down on to the ice. Water was creeping over the edge of some of the cracks already.

"We can't risk kicking the ball along the ground," said Louise. "If we lose it in the water, the game's over."

"And move as lightly as possible," warned Frankie. He saw Charlie already pressing forward, and chipped the ball towards him. Charlie caught it, but stumbled a little. His weight sent more cracks across the ice, leaving him stranded on the island. The Krampus's laughter rang out.

"To me!" said Louise, rushing upfield.

Charlie hurled the ball towards
her, and Louise dropped on to her
knees in a slide. The ice broke up
behind her but she managed to get
her head to the ball and it spun up
into the air. Max scampered after
it as Frankie skidded towards the
goal. With every step, he felt the
ice break up more. A huge crack had

opened ahead. He saw Max reach the ball just as it landed. It bounced off his front paws and sailed high over the pitch. Max yelped in fear as he slid into a patch of freezing water with a splosh. He came up, choking and splashing wildly. "I'm . . . all right!" he barked. "Go get him, Frankie!"

Frankie heard the Krampus bark another laugh. A stretch of water had opened up ahead, scattered with broken islands of ice. He couldn't reach the ball unless he jumped. He'd need perfect timing.

He raced over to the edge and leapt off, landing on the next patch of ice and almost toppling. It glided across the water like a surfboard just as the ball plummeted towards him.

"Go, Frankie!" shouted Charlie.

Frankie brought his leg around and kicked the ball right off the top of his foot. It shot through the air . . . towards the post!

The Krampus dived athletically, reaching with the fingertips of Charlie's gloves, but the ball bounced off the inside of the post and into the goal.

"Supergoal!" said Louise.

Frankie hopped from ice-sheet to ice-sheet, until he reached Max,

who was frantically paddling in the water. He fished out the drenched dog.

"It . . . t . . . t's a l . . . l . . . lot c . . . colder than the neighbours' pond," said Max. He shook his fur and icy droplets flew off.

"You lose," said Frankie, turning to the Krampus.

"I won't give them back," said the Krampus, stamping his hooves. "I won't, won't, *won't*!"

"Yes, you will," said a voice from behind the goal. A figure stepped out.

"Robin!" said Louise.

Frankie's anger surged. "What

are you doing here?" he said. "You betrayed us. You and that reindeer almost buried us in an avalanche."

Robin looked at his feet, just the same way Kevin did when he was ashamed. "I'm sorry," he said. "I chose the wrong side. I thought the avalanche would throw you off the trail — I never meant any serious harm."

"Hold on," said the Krampus. "Sorry to interrupt, but you seem to have forgotten, Robert — I'm the boss here!"

"It's Robin, actually," said Charlie.

"Frankie and his friends have

shown me the true meaning of Christmas again," said Robin. "I can't just stand back and watch. They are brave and kind. You are just a miserable old goat."

"I am the Krampus!" their enemy roared. But Frankie could see the desperation in his eyes. "The Bringer of Winter, Ruiner of Christmas, Scourge of Happiness."

"Blah–blah–blah," said Louise. She and Charlie had reached the goal and surrounded the Krampus. Frankie joined them, leaping from his floating section of ice with Max in his arms.

The Krampus looked at all of

them, then tore off his goalie gloves and hurled them on the ground. "Useless things."

"A bad keeper blames his gloves," said Charlie.

The Krampus turned and ran away into the tunnel behind him.

"G . . . good riddance," said Max. He was shivering violently, and Frankie saw icicles starting to form in his fur.

"Come on," said Robin. "There's a back entrance with a sled waiting. I have a blanket in there."

Frankie began to pile the presents back into the sack. "We need to take these with us," he reminded the others. They all came to help.

"I'm sorry I tricked you," said the elf quietly. "The Krampus promised me presents all year round, and I was greedy. I should have known that presents are only special if they're given willingly."

"I sort of understand," said Frankie. "At least you came back to help us."

With the gifts all loaded again, Frankie tied the end of the sack, and readied himself to heave. But to his surprise, the sack was very light, and he could easily pull it along.

"Christmas magic," said Robin, as he led them along another tunnel. "How else do you think Santa could deliver all his presents?"

They came out into daylight, where a single reindeer stood hitched to a sled. "Thank goodness you won," the reindeer said.

"You must be Maradona," said Charlie. "What's your excuse for turning against Santa?"

The reindeer lowered his head. "I was fed up of being at the back of the crew all the time. Pelé was always promising me a promotion, but it never happened. Then the Krampus said I could have my own sled. I didn't know I'd just be pulling him around everywhere."

"Just because you're not playing in front of goal, doesn't mean you're not an important part of the team," said Louise. Frankie smiled — he remembered their coach Mr Donald saying the same thing to her once.

"Sure you can lift us all?" he asked, loading on the sack.

"Hop on," said Maradona with a wink.

CHAPTER 9

Maradona shot across the sky in
soaring glides and sudden swoops,
his hooves leaving trails of sparkles.
Frankie clung on for dear life. It
was scary, but a lot of fun as well,
just like a roller coaster.

They passed high over the
entrance to the ice caves, the site of

the avalanche and the great crack of the crevasse.

When they arrived back at Santa's palace, Maradona dipped his nose and brought the sled down for a smooth landing. The palace seemed to glow behind its frosted windows, and several sleds were lined up outside, each with a crew of reindeer harnessed and ready to go. Elves were loading sacks on to the sleds, while at a long trestle table more were serving cups of steaming drinks.

Max, still wrapped in a blanket in the back of the sled, raised his eyebrows. "Can I smell marshmallows?" he asked, nose twitching.

Frankie saw more elves toasting something over a fire. "I think so," he said, taking in the scene.

People rushed over towards Frankie and his friends.

"They're back!" cried a young elf.

The doors burst open and Santa came shambling over the snow. He'd changed into his traditional costume of red fur with white trim, but he wasn't wearing his hat yet. His trousers looked very baggy, held up with a black belt around his slim waist.

When the elves saw the sack of

presents in the sled, they broke out into clapping and cheers.

The other reindeer emerged from their stable and gathered around Maradona. "He's got some explaining to do," Louise whispered in Frankie's ear.

Frankie jumped off the sled as a group of elves rushed forward and gathered up the sack full of presents.

"Well done!" boomed Santa. "I was beginning to worry!"

"So was I," said Frankie. "The Krampus is a difficult opponent, that's for sure."

"Hot chocolate and

marshmallows for Frankie's team,"
said one of the elves.

"I'll get them," said Robin,
rushing off to one of the serving
tables.

Santa Claus laughed. "I'd say
their feat deserves a lot more
than that," he said. "How about a
Christmas wish?"

"A wish?" said Charlie, eyes lighting up.

"Anything you want!" said Santa. "You've saved Christmas for a lot of football-mad children."

Frankie frowned, deep in thought.

"Wait!" said Charlie. "No one say anything. People always make silly wishes without thinking, when really they should wish for countless wishes . . ."

"I wish we could go home," said Max, who was still huddled in a blanket on the back of the sled. "I'm freez . . ."

The snowy landscape vanished.

". . . zing," Max finished.

Frankie looked around. He and his friends were back in his bedroom. It was still dark outside, but his clock read 6 a.m. Not long until morning.

"Oh great!" said Charlie. "What did I just say?"

Frankie realised his snow globe was resting on his windowsill once more. The flakes were still, the glass was clear, and nothing moved inside. He suddenly felt very tired.

"Let's go to sleep," he said.

Max curled up happily on the end of his bed as Frankie peeled off his layers and climbed beneath

the sheets. Charlie and Louise
took off their hats and scarves and
scrambled into their sleeping bags.

Charlie shook his head at Max,
before closing his eyes. Frankie
couldn't help smiling to himself.
Max had robbed Charlie of endless
wishes, but it didn't really matter.
Lots of other wishes were about to
come true soon.

The following night, Frankie
tossed and turned under his
duvet. It was always the same
on Christmas Eve. But this
time it wasn't excitement about
Christmas Day that kept him

awake. He was still thinking about their adventures in Lapland. He wondered if Charlie and Louise were struggling to sleep as well, back in their own homes.

Something else bothered Frankie too.

Pelé the reindeer had said he'd found them because of the magic football, but where was it? Even with Louise and Charlie helping him look all around the house that morning, it was nowhere to be found. Kevin still wouldn't tell him what he'd done with it.

Frankie heard a shuffling sound from downstairs. Perhaps Max was trying to get at the mince pie on the table beside the TV. He rolled over and closed his eyes.

There was another noise, like a grunt. It sounded as if someone was struggling.

Frankie climbed out of bed and crept to his bedroom door. The landing outside was quiet, and he could hear his dad snoring. Kevin's door was shut too.

The sounds are coming from downstairs, he thought. Frankie padded down the stairs, and into the living room. Lights twinkled on the Christmas tree. Max was standing beside the fireplace. The hair on the back of his neck was bristling.

"What is it, boy?" Frankie asked.

Max pointed his snout at the hearth.

Two boots dropped into the ashes in the grate, followed by a cloud of soot. Santa Claus clambered out with a sack in one hand. Miraculously, he was completely clean.

"Greetings once more!" he boomed.

"Shhh!" said Frankie, pressing his finger to his lips and casting an anxious look back at the door. "My family are asleep."

"Ah. Right you are," said Santa.
"Bit of a job getting down that
chimney. It was blocked with this.'

From behind his back he drew
out a black, deflated shape.

"The magic football!" said
Frankie. He guessed what had
happened. *Kevin must have kicked
it on to the roof and it fell down the
chimney.*

Santa opened his sack and took
out a few presents, placing them
under the tree in the corner of the
room. One looked like just the right
size for a box containing football
boots. "Must dash," he said. "I'm
going to Charlie and Louise's homes

next. Have a Merry Christmas." He gave Frankie a wink. "Thank you for everything you did."

"Thanks," said Frankie. He hesitated, then asked the question that was still bothering him. "What will happen with the Krampus?" Santa's enemy was still out there in Lapland, somewhere.

Santa shook his head. "Don't worry about him," he said, placing a hand on Frankie's shoulder. "Maradona feels so guilty about what he did, he's determined to keep the Krampus away. He'll never have the chance to ruin Christmas again."

Santa turned back to the chimney

when he spied the mince pie.
He plucked it up and looked at it
longingly, then patted his stomach.
"Better not," he said. He held
the pie to Max, who snatched it
between his teeth and swallowed it,
barely chewing.

Frankie wasn't exactly sure how
he did it, but Santa managed to get
into the hearth again just as the
door opened and Kevin wandered
in rubbing his eyes. His hair was
sticking up in all sorts of directions.
"What's all the noise, Frankie?" he
said. His eyes widened as Santa's
legs wiggled in the chimney. "Argh!
What's that?"

"Keep it down," said Frankie.

"We're being robbed!" cried Kevin. "Call the police!"

"We're not being robbed," said Frankie. "It's Santa Claus." He seemed to be having problems climbing back up – his boots were still wiggling in the air.

Footsteps came down the stairs and Frankie panicked. How was he going to explain this one?

His mum and dad came into the room, both wearing their dressing gowns.

"Boys, it's very late," said his dad. "You should both be in bed."

"But . . ." said Kevin, pointing

a shaking finger at the fireplace. "Santa . . ."

Frankie shot a glance at the fireplace. The boots had vanished.

Their dad rolled his eyes. "Come on Kev," he said. "You're much too old for stories like that."

Frankie grinned at Max. "Yeah, don't be daft, Kevin. Who believes in Father Christmas? It's for little kids, you said."

As he left his brother scowling and headed upstairs to bed, he heard his mum muttering, "Look at all those presents, John! Are they from Auntie Brenda?"

"No idea," said his dad. "Back to bed for me."

Frankie grinned, thinking of his new football boots waiting under the tree. He couldn't wait to try them on and go to the park with his friends.

And now he had the magic football back as well.

This will be the best Christmas ever!

ACKNOWLEDGEMENTS

Many thanks to everyone at Little,
Brown Book Group; Neil Blair, Zoe
King, Daniel Teweles and all at The
Blair Partnership; Luella Wright
for bringing my characters to life;
special thanks to Michael Ford
for all his wisdom and patience;

and to Steve Kutner for being a great friend and for all his help and guidance, not just with the book but with everything.

FRANKIE'S MAGIC FOOTBALL

Did you know?

Unlike China and Brazil, Lapland isn't a country. It is a region of Finland! The native Sami people have their own flag, which is flown on certain days of the year instead of the Finnish flag.

Could you be a winner, like Frankie?

Take a look at the pictures in this book. Somewhere, we have hidden a miniature Sami flag, just like this one:

Can you find it?

For the chance to win an exclusive Frankie's Magic Football goodie bag, write down the page number this secret image appears on then visit www.frankiesmagicfootball.com/competitions and ask a grown up to help you fill in the form.

Once you've completed your entry, you will be able to download a template to colour in your own Sami flag.

This competition is open to all readers. Closing date is 31.12.2014. For full terms and conditions, see the website.

Frankie wishes you all good luck.

Remember, everyone has talent!

FRANKIE'S MAGIC FOOTBALL

Have you read all of these adventures?

Tick the ones you have!

FRANKIE'S MAGIC FOOTBALL WEBSITE

Have you had a chance to check out **frankiesmagicfootball.com** yet?

Get involved in **competitions**, find out **news** and **updates** about the series, play **games** and watch **videos** featuring the author, **Frank Lampard!**

Visit the site to join **Frankie's FC** today!